W9-AZK-574

This book belongs to:

JE
Spetter, Jung-Hee.
Lily and Trooper's fall
                8.95

DEC 0 2 2008

Story Link®
Program

For Ilse, Maya and Soon-Dae

Library of Congress Cataloging-in-Publication Data

Spetter, Jung-Hee, 1969-
    [Natte neuzen. English]
    Lily and Trooper's fall / Jung-Hee Spetter. — 1st American ed.
        p.   cm.
    Summary: A little girl and her dog have fun playing outdoors
    on a blustery fall day.
    ISBN 1-886910-38-3 (hardcover)
    [1. Autumn—Fiction. 2. Dogs—Fiction]   I. Title.
    PZ7.S7515Li   1999
    [E]—dc21   98-27972

Copyright © 1998 by Lemniscaat b.v. Rotterdam
Originally published in the Netherlands under the title *Natte neuzen*
by Lemniscaat b.v. Rotterdam
All rights reserved
Printed and bound in Belgium
First American edition

Jung-Hee Spetter

Lily and Trooper's Fall

Front Street 8 Lemniscaat

Asheville, North Carolina

This book belongs to:

MID-CONTINENT PUBLIC LIBRARY

3 0001 00528935 2

"Mmmm. I slept like a log, Trooper."

"Trooper, look at the leaves. It's fall."

"I love it when the leaves fall!"

"Let's make a pile and jump in it!"

"I bet you can't find me!" – "Woof woof!"

"Uh-oh! It's raining. Let's run."

"Brrrrr!"

"This time I'm bringing my umbrella . . ."

". . . and wearing my boots!"

"Sailing, sailing . . ."

"Shiver me timbers!"

"There goes the sail!"

"Brrrrr!" – "Woof woof!"

"Up up and away!"

"Whoops!"

"Fetch, Trooper!"

"Good dog, Trooper. Good dog!"

"Let's go for a ride."

"Look out below! Here we come!"

"Oomph! – "Woof!"

"Aaaaaargh!"

SPLOOSH!

"Once upon a time there was a girl and her dog . . ."

"Good night, Trooper. I love you."